ONE MONSTER AFTER ANOTHER

GINGHAM DOG
PRESS

Columbus, Ohio

ONE MONSTER
AFTER ANOTHER

Written and illustrated by Mercer Mayer

McGraw Hill **Children's Publishing**

A Big Tuna Trading Company, LLC/
J.R. Sansevere Book

Send all inquiries to:
McGraw-Hill Children's Publishing • 8787 Orion Place • Columbus, Ohio 43240-4027

www.MHKids.com   Printed in the United States of America.

1-57768-688-8 (HC) • 1-57768-858-9 (PB)

Library of Congress Cataloging-in-Publication Data on file with the publisher.

2 3 4 5 6 7 8 9 PHXBK 07 06 05 04 03

One day Sally Ann wrote a letter to her best friend Lucy Jane. She put it in an envelope and put the envelope into her mailbox.

But before the mailman came, a Stamp-Collecting Trollusk crept up to the mailbox, stole the letter, and gabbled away with a smirk on his snerk.

But before the Stamp-Collecting Trollusk could tear off the stamp and collect it, a Letter-Eating Bombanat flew out of Nowhere and snapped up the letter.

Over the Blue Ocean of Bubbly Goo the Letter-Eating Bombanat flew.

But before he could find a nice place to settle down and eat the letter, a Bombanat-Munching Grumley reached up out of the goo and grabbed him.

But before the Bombanat-Munching Grumley could slither down into the sea for a nice Bombanat lunch–SNAP–he was snagged by a big fishing net and hauled wiggly-squiggly on board a fishing boat.

But before the fishing boat could reach land, it was struck by a
Furious-Floating Ice-Ferg. SCRUNNCCCHHH!! As the ship went
down, the captain quickly stuffed a note into a bottle. He pushed
in the letter for good measure, and then threw it into the ocean.

$\mathcal{B}$ut before anyone could find the bottle, a Wild-'n-Windy Typhoonigator came storming along, sucking up everything in its path. It sucked up the whole Blue Ocean of Bubbly Goo– the bottle, too–then blew itself away.

By morning, the Wild-'n-Windy Typhoonigator was full, so full of fishing boats, bottles, and bubbly goo, that it had to let go.

Down fell the letter which was in the bottle which was in the Blue Ocean of Bubbly Goo. Down fell the bottle, KER-PLOP, right on the head of a Paper-Munching Yalapappus who lived on the edge of Nowhere.
The bottle broke, tinkle-plinkle, and out fell the Captain's note and the letter. The Yalapappus smiled. It had been such a long time since he'd had any nice paper to munch.

Gleefully he grabbed the Captain's note and munched it. But before he could munch the letter, too, the Stamp-Collecting Trollusk, who just happened to be passing by, snatched the letter in his snerk and ran away.

The Paper-Munching Yalapappus trundled after him, shouting and loudly grimming.

Suddenly, out of the sky swooped the Letter-Eating Bombanat. SNIP! He snapped up the letter.

ut before the Letter-Eating Bombanat could eat the letter, he was snared in a net, caught, FLIP-FLOP, by the Bombanat-Collecting Grithix.

he Grithix, as everybody knows, is a Bombanat collector, not a letter collector. He had no use for someone else's mail, so he did what anybody should do with a lost letter. He mailed it! The Paper-Munching Yalapappus and the Stamp-Collecting Trollusk and the Letter-Eating Bombanat watched helplessly as the Grithix opened an official-looking mailbox and dropped the letter in.

And before they could steal the mailbox, a mailman
rode up on an official-looking motorcycle.
"Stop!" he cried. "Unhand that official mailbox!"
There was nothing they could do. After all, he was an official mailman.

The official mailman opened the official mailbox and
took out all the letters. Away he rode, leaving the Yalapappus
and the Trollusk waving their paws in the air and wailing at the
Bombanat-Collecting Grithix.

The Grithix didn't care a snickle. Paying no attention to all the noise, he walked home, clasping the Letter-Eating Bombanat firmly under one arm.

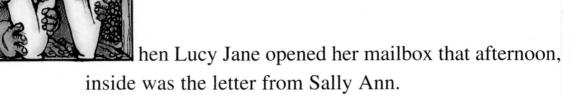hen Lucy Jane opened her mailbox that afternoon, inside was the letter from Sally Ann.

Dear Lucy Jane,
Nothing exciting ever happens around here.
Please come and visit.
Your Best Friend,
Sally Ann